Chase,
The Rapping Girl

* * *

Blaike Wellington

Illustration by
Chris Lincoln

BLAIKE WELLINGTON PUBLISHING

Blaike Wellington Publishing
925 W Baseline Rd Ste105-E8
Tempe, AZ/85283
www.blaikewellington.com

Publisher's Note: This is a work of fiction. Names, characters, places, and incidents are a product of the author's imagination. Locales and public names are sometimes used for atmospheric purposes. Any resemblance to actual people, living or dead, or to businesses, companies, events, institutions, or locales is completely coincidental.

Book design © 2017 BookDesignTemplates.com

Ordering Information: Special discounts are available on quantity purchases by corporations, associations, and others. For details, contact the publisher at the address above.

Tempe / Blaike Wellington — First Edition
ISBN 978-1-7335226-0-1

Printed in the United States of America

Dedication

I want to dedicate *Chase, The Rapping Girl* to everyone! I believe there is a rapping girl inside of all of us. Rapping may not be your gift, however, there is something inside of you that can and will be a blessing to us all. I encourage you to find the light inside of yourself and bring it out. Let the world see who you are and the greatness inside of you.

Contents

* * *

Thanks and Acknowledgments

* * *

I want to give thanks to my Lord and Savior Jesus Christ. I truly believe with the power of God, I can do all things through Christ who strengthens me. Many years ago, it was prophesized that I would become a writer. I am so grateful to see the prophecy come to fruition. God has truly blessed me over the years, and I am grateful for His love, favor, and glory over my life.

Through this journey I have to give thanks to all of my family members: my parents: Isaiah Dickerson, Sarah Dickerson, Timothy Wellington, and Angel Wellington; my siblings: Branden Wellington, Isaiah Dickerson Jr., Timothy Wellington Jr., Nazhane Wellington, Ikeem Dickerson, Timeon Wellington, and

Alexander Wellington; my grandparents, aunts, uncles, and cousins, extended family, and my friends for all their help, support, and encouragement. Thank you for believing in me and my dreams.

I want to personally thank my immediate family for reading my story over and over again and providing me feedback and encouragement. I say with all laughs and smiles, I know that I was getting on your nerves, but I am so grateful that I have such an amazing, supportive family to help me along the way. I personally would like to thank my mother, Sarah, for all of her help, support, and encouragement. Mom, you are my inspiration. I am blessed to have you as a mother, and I am so grateful for you.

I want to give thanks to Chris Lincoln for providing me with amazing illustrations. You have truly brought my imagination to life. Also, I want to thank everyone who has played a part in putting *Chase, The Rapping Girl* together and making it great!

Last but not least, Thank you to all who have purchased *Chase, The Rapping Girl*. You are truly special to me, and I am grateful for your support. I hope that *Chase, The Rapping Girl,* helps you find you gifts and talent and be the best person you can be. Don't be afraid of letting your inner light shine bright. You were wonderfully made, and you can do anything that you put your mind to.

Love you all,
Blaike Wellington

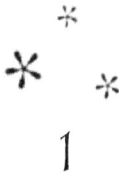

1

The Dinner Table!

Today is just a typical, boring school day like any other.

Nothing unusual or exciting has happened. It's four o'clock, and as we're dismissed from class, it's time to walk home. It's the perfect time for me to listen to my music and forget about the uneventful school day. Don't get me wrong, I love learning new things in school, especially English, but I'm often bored because I do not have many friends.

There is only one person that talks to me. Her name is Kourtney, and she lives a couple of houses down from me, so we always walk to and from school together. We are the only girls our age that live on our block. We do not talk much, but I do like her. I know she would talk more to me if I opened up a little better, but I am so shy and don't have much to say. One time, on the way home from school, I asked her one question and her answer turned into a life story. She didn't stop talking until we reached her house, and she said my name, Chase, at least seven times. It was an overwhelming experience. So now, I just listen to my music.

As I walk into the house, I get right into my usual routine: make a sandwich with some chips on the side and start my homework. I have to finish my English essay by turning the outline into a final draft. It's a persuasive essay on "why six graders need different options for recess." This is a good topic to write about because I am not a fan of recess. It's the same thing every day... kids playing basketball, chasing each other around the playground, or girls gossiping and flirting with the boys. Recess should be a fun time for everyone, and our typical recess does not relate to kids like me. Listening to music is always fun for me, so I can imagine a DJ outside on the playground playing everyone's favorite songs or the latest jams on the radio. If I had recess my way, everyone would be dancing and singing. It would feel like it's a party going on. That would be a great recess!

With my homework finally finished, it's time for my chores. Doing chores doesn't bother me since I can listen to my music. Old school rap music is my favorite, especially Rob Base and DJ E-Z Rock. The new music on the radio is cool, but the old beats get me excited. The old beats make me want to get up and dance all night long. They are also easy to rap along with. All I ever want to do is write rhymes to the beats. I like to study words in the dictionary so that I can have more to say in my raps. My parents can't know that I like to rap because I am afraid they will not approve. They do not like rap music, and they do not let me listen to it.

As I am listening to my music and writing down rhymes, my mom opens up my door. "Chase, I can tell you have your music up loud again. I knocked on the door several times. Is your homework done and school clothes ready for tomorrow?" my mom asks sounding a little annoyed.

"Yes, ma'am."

"Okay, wash your hands. Dinner is ready," my mom says while closing the door.

How annoying! I do not like dinner time. Dinner time is when my family talks about their day. My parents ask me the same questions every time, and I end up giving the same answers. You would think they would get the point by now, but I guess not.

After I wash my hands, I get to the dinner table, and unsurprisingly, it's the same routine as usual. My mom and dad are talking about their day at work as they normally do, while my four-year-old brother Chandler plays with his food and makes a mess. Watching my brother play with his food is the best part about dinner. He is funny and the coolest four-year-old boy ever! He is always happy and never gets on my nerves. I hear horror stories all the time from the kids at school about their little brothers, but Chandler is nothing like them. He laughs all day even when nothing is particularly funny. Chandler and I have a special connection. He understands me and I understand him. As close as we are, I never rap my music around my brother. Sometimes I let him come into my room and listen to music with me. It's weird I connect more with a four-year-old kid than I do with people my own age. Sometimes I wonder if it's because we both have such large imaginations.

I find myself drifting off into daydreams all the time. I like to imagine myself performing on stage, rapping the coolest song, wearing the coolest clothes, and the crowd screaming my name. While daydreaming, I often forget where I am at... especially at the dinner table. Just when I drift off into a day dream, I hear a bang at the table, my brother playing cheerfully, and it causes me to blink and snap back to reality. My dad is staring at me curiously. I think, *"Please do not ask me about my day,"* but I already know what is coming.

"Chase, how was your day at school, baby girl?" my father asks as he picks up his lemonade.

"My day went well. Nothing unusual happened," I say looking down at my plate, playing with my peas, counting down the seconds for this conversation to end.

"How is your friend next door doing? I notice that when you are walking home, you and Kourtney don't talk to each other much," my mom notes.

Wow! This is a change in the usual routine of questions. They never ask me about Kourtney. I wonder where this is going?

"Kourtney is doing well," I reply, making sure to use proper English, so my mother doesn't feel the need to correct me. My mother does not like it if I use slang. I must speak proper at all times in her presence.

"Baby girl, why don't you talk to Kourtney? It seems like she wants to be your friend," my mother continues.

"I talk to her, but I just like to listen to my music when I walk home from school."

"Now I did not buy you that music player so you could avoid socializing with your peers," my mom says staring at me with a stern look on her face.

"Honey, it is okay. She can listen to her music. She likes music, just like her dad," my dad responds with a big smile for my mother.

Mom has no comment because she wants to avoid arguing with my dad. All I can do is smile. When it comes to music, I can count on my dad to take my side. That's why my dad and I are so close; we connect through music. It's annoying my mom doesn't like me listening to music outside the house. All she wants me to do is make friends. Even when I don't listen to my music on my headphones, my classmates still don't speak me. She says I am making excuses. She doesn't understand because she is not into music like me and my dad, and she was prom queen. She was Miss Popular at her high school and always had lots of friends growing up. My mom wants me to be the way she was at my age, but I live in a different world than she does.

Kourtney is the only person I can talk to at school because she lets me be myself. When I am with her, she does all the talking. In fact, it's an unspoken agreement that works out great for the both of us.

I'm glad dinner is over, and I feel like I just came out of an interrogation room. To my mom, not having a social life is a crime, and I am the number one suspect. I am ready to relax and get into my personal writing zone. I have a notebook just for rhymes that I keep hidden underneath my mattress. My mom will never look under there. Whenever I get into the zone and start writing rhymes, I lose all track of time.

Oh no! It's ten o'clock! I better go to bed before my parents come in.

2

It's Just a Dream

"GO Chase! Go Chase!" the crowd is screaming out my name.

The lights are bright and shining in my face. The music is so loud it could burst your ear drums. All of a sudden, I hear this loud beeping sound that is messing up the mix.

"Chase! Chase! Wake up and turn off that alarm!" my mom yells.

"Yes ma'am," I reply with a sigh, turning off the alarm.

Wow, that dream felt real! I could've sworn I was there, standing on stage, rapping to the crowd. I didn't feel nervous or shy. It was definitely a dream.

Dreaming of rapping in a sold-out show has me in a good mood this morning. While my music is playing, I can't stop dancing around the room. Dang, if only the dream was real! Rapping on stage in front of a lot of people, including my mom, is like winning the lottery. It's possible, but the odds are extremely low. I just need to get over my fears. More than anything, I fear my mom's opinion. I can see her face now. She would give me a never-ending speech until my ears started to bleed. Not rapping is better than hearing her go on and on negatively about rap music. Thinking about what she would say brings me down. I am going to keep thinking about my dream, so I can get back into a good mood.

Soon I'm ready to get out of the house and be at school. As I walk out the door, I turn around to say goodbye to my mom, and she is giving me a look.

"Remember what I said about that music player, Chase," my mom speaks in a serious tone from the table where she's drinking her coffee.

"Yes ma'am!" I agree, closing the door and

rolling my eyes. Of course I closed the door before rolling my eyes. I wouldn't dare do it in front of my mom. It would be stupid or crazy of me to do something like that!

While standing outside waiting for Kourtney to leave her house, I wonder to myself if I should tell Kourtney about my dream. Running out of the house, her energy is on full blast, which is normal for her. She is always hyper, but today her energy is on another level. Thank God I am in a good mood and have a little more patience today than usual. I'll just have to tell her about my dream another time.

"Hey, Chase!" Kourtney says while running towards me.

"Hi, Kourtney," I reply, putting my music player in my backpack.

"What! No music today? What is going on?" Kourtney asks.

"My mom doesn't want me listening to my music all the time."

"Oh speaking of music! Guess what I did last night!" Kourtney's excitement is undeniable.

"My parents had friends and family over, and I got to stay up super late. They had their music playing, and my cousins and I were up all night dancing. I had so much fun!"

"What kind of music was your family playing?" I ask enthusiastically.

"They played a lot of old hip hop songs. Do you know that song by Rob Base and DJ E-Z Rock, called 'It Takes Two?'"

"That is my favorite song!" I yell out.

Before I can catch myself, I just start rapping the song. I rap the entire first verse and hook, and Kourtney starts rapping the song with me while dancing around in circles.

"Wow Chase, you know how to rap! I have never seen this side of you before."

I'm embarrassed, and I can't stop blushing. "I'm sorry," I say with my head hanging down.

"Why are you sorry? You sound great! Oh my gosh! I have an idea!" Kourtney is literally jumping up and down with excitement.

Oh no, Kourtney and her ideas. I can only imagine what she is about to say. Please God, do not let her suggest something crazy. This is why I do not talk to her for long periods of time. She gets too excited, and she starts talking crazy.

"You should rap in the school talent show! You would do great!"

With my eyes wide, tongue tied, heart beating fast, I am speechless. I never thought I would be in a talent show, let alone rap in front of people. Just thinking about it is giving me goose bumps. Plus, if she heard me rap, my mom would fall out of her seat, faint, wake up, and give me a lecture, then faint again. Just the thought of her reaction is making my stomach hurt.

"Thank you, but no thank you. I don't want to rap in the talent show," I say in a soft tone.

"Well, if you change your mind, let me know. I'll do the talent show with you if you are too shy to do it by yourself. You know I can dance!" Kourtney says while dabbing.

As we are walking inside the school, I can't get my mind to focus on schoolwork because

I am thinking about Kourtney's idea. She does know how to dance. In fact, she dances so much it gets on my nerves at times. She is the best dancer in school, and she is pretty popular.

Ring! Ring! Ring!

Oh shoot! That's the bell. I've never been late to class before. All this talent show talk has me bugging.

"Good morning class! I have an announcement for you. The school talent show is coming up, and if you want to be in the show, you must sign up by Friday," my homeroom and English teacher, Mrs. Harper, announces.

Oh no! Today is Wednesday. That means I only have two days to decide if I am going to participate in the talent show. A decision needs to be made quickly. Wait a minute... I can't even believe I am thinking about rapping in the talent show. What am I thinking!? Maybe it's that dream I had this morning, but I'm not brave enough to do this! I can't rap in the show for three reasons. One, I am way too shy to do it. Two, my mother would have a nervous breakdown and pass out. And the third reason is my mother would wake up and pass out again. Nobody has time for her dramatic scenes. If I ask her permission to rap in the show, she will probably say no and end up taking my music player away. It's bad enough I don't have many friends. I cannot let her take my music too. Music is all I have!

Maybe I need to think more rationally. My mom is not a mean woman, so she might let me do it, but she always gets annoyed with my dad when he plays music. I feel a headache coming on! No more thinking about this talent show. It's starting to make me upset. There's no way I'm rapping on stage in front of my entire school and mom. End of discussion.

3

The Journal Assignment

Every morning my class has to write a journal entry.

Mrs. Harper gives us one hour to write our response to the writing prompt. Mrs. Harper sets a timer, and as soon as the timer goes off, we have to put our pencils down. I love journal writing time because sometimes we get to have a free day and write whatever we want. Sometimes Mrs. Harper reads our journal assignments, and sometimes she doesn't. She knows that rapping is my passion because I am always writing down verses to songs. Knowing Mrs. Harper, she probably calls it poetry.

For our journal assignment today, she wants us to write about our talent and what makes us unique. Really! Of all the things there is to write about, she wants us to write about our talent. She must be feeling the talent show spirit. I am definitely *not* feeling the talent show spirit. I just want to write verses and rhymes.

I put my pencil to paper and begin to write: "What makes me a unique rapper, I'm really not sure. Maybe it's my rhymes or my swag. Or it could be my look, since I don't look like a typical rapper. In fact, some may say I look like a nerd. But I am a cool nerd. I think being a nerd is what makes me different from other rappers. I am a nerd with swag. Because I like to read and write, I have a larger vocabulary to work with. I am unstoppable with lyrics, and I know how to freestyle rap off the top of my head.

"The only problem I have is fear. I am afraid to show people my nerdy swag, that side of me I never show. What if they don't accept me? What if my mom doesn't approve? People may not look at me the same if they know I rap. If only I was as brave as professional rappers. Regardless of my fear, I know I am different from your typical rapper and have a lot of unique things to say."

Bing! Bing! Bing!

"That is the timer, class. Pencils down," Mrs. Harper instructs everyone. "So, who are my three volunteers willing to share their journal writing today?"

Mrs. Harper always calls on the first three people to raise their hand. If there are no volunteers, then she will call on people randomly. Luckily for me, I never get called on. This is the worst part about writing time because I hold my breath until the third person is chosen.

A girl named Erica is the first to share her work. I am not surprised because she always volunteers first. She is the teacher's pet and our school's most annoying student. I never listen to what she has to say.

Jonathon is the next to share. Jonathon is Mr. Arrogant, and he thinks he is so cool. His talent is rapping, and he thinks he is the best rapper because he won the talent show last year. But really, he only won because he didn't have any competition.

The last person to share is Kourtney. I knew Kourtney was going to share because she likes attention. Everyone knows Kourtney's talent is dancing. Kourtney feels she is unique because she has taken every kind of dance lesson you can think of! Her mom acts likes the moms off of the TV show "Dance Moms." She might actually be worse than them.

I am so glad I have classmates like Teacher's Pet, Mr. Arrogant, and Ms. Attention Seeker! It makes it easy to avoid having to read my writing out loud. Just when I think I am in the clear, Mrs. Harper calls my name to share my work. What is going on today? I am shocked. She never calls on anybody after she gets her three volunteers. This lady is trying to set me up for embarrassment.

"Chase Steward, what is your talent and what makes your talent unique?" Mrs. Harper asks with a huge smile on her face.

I feel my face turning red, my legs are shaking, and I cannot seem to swallow or speak.

"Umm, Umm, Mrs. Harper, I'm sorry, but I rather not share my journal assignment with the class," I reply nervously.

"You know the rules, Chase. If you do not share when being called on, I take five minutes off your recess," Mrs. Harper says with a confused, but serious face.

"Yes ma'am," I mumble with my head buried

on the desk top, trying to keep myself from crying.

Out of nowhere, Mr. Arrogant Jonathon, yells out, "She don't have no talent! The only talent she has is putting her head down! What a nerd!"

The entire class starts laughing. Amidst the laughter, Kourtney yells across the room, "Shut up, Jonathon! You don't know what you're talking about! For your information, Chase knows how to rap, something you will never know how to do!"

The class laughs louder.

"Ok, sure! And I am Ariana Grande!" Jonathon replies sarcastically in a girly voice.

"Everyone stop talking!" Mrs. Harper yells. "That is five minutes off from everyone's recess."

Wow! Mrs. Harper never yells. She must be really mad. Now I have ten minutes off of my recess. I don't care about losing the time because I don't do anything anyway. All I do is watch Kourtney dance, or write songs in my notebook. Although, I don't care about losing the time, I am angry at Kourtney for telling everyone I know how to rap. She has such a big mouth. I'm thankful she stuck up for me, but she has no idea how embarrassed I feel right now.

4

The Talk

Everyone is sitting against the fence in silence at the beginning of recess.

It's awkward every time the entire class loses recess time. Everyone stands in one spot looking around at each other or staring off into space as if they are about to take a mug shot. It's humiliating. The teachers act like guards waiting for someone to talk so they can add more time to their prison sentence, or should I say recess. I think I've read the book *Holes* too many times, except we are not digging holes, and I don't see how I am building character standing in one spot in silence.

The whistle blows and Mrs. Harper says to go play at recess. On the other hand, I have five more minutes left on my sentence... I mean recess. Oh no, Mrs. Harper is walking towards me. She never talks to me during recess, so I can only imagine that she is about to give me "the talk."

"Hello, Chase!"

"Hi, Mrs. Harper."

"Miss Steward, I am curious, why did you not want to share your writing assignment with the class?"

I put my head down and hunch my shoulders.

"Miss Steward, please use your words."

"I was scared, Mrs. Harper," I reply in a soft tone.

"What are you afraid of?"

"I was scared everyone would laugh at me," I speak with my head still facing the ground.

"Chase, I read all of your journal assignments. In most of your free-write assignments you talk about listening to music and writing songs. I know that you like to rap. You write poetry all the time, and you're very good at it. The kids may have laughed at you, but some of the most talented people in the world were made fun of. Are there any other reasons why you did not want to share?"

This lady has been playing us. I did not know

that she was reading all the journal assignments. She has us thinking our journal is a private journal, like a diary, and all this time she knew that I rap. What an invasion of privacy! Now she is trying to have a therapy session. This is why I stay out of trouble, so I won't get "the talk" from her or my parents.

"My mom does not like rap music, so I know she would get upset if she found out I like rap music, and that I like to rap," I confess.

"Have you talked to your mom about it?" Mrs. Harper asks with concerned tone.

"No, I haven't. I am afraid she won't like the kind of music I like to write."

This woman is nuts if she thinks I am about to tell my parents I rap. She doesn't know my parents. My dad may not be as mad, but my mom would fly off the handle!

"Chase, look at me! It is okay to show your mom and your peers your true self. It's time for you to stop hiding behind your notebook and let everyone get to know the real Chase. Everyone may not like you, but it doesn't matter what they think about you. It matters what you think about yourself. You have a chance to shine, and I would love to see you perform in the talent show," Mrs. Harper says with a big smile on her face.

With ten minutes left, I decide to keep to myself for the remainder of recess. I'm still upset with Kourtney, so I don't want to talk to her. I can't believe she told the class I know how to rap. She only heard me rap one song, and it wasn't even my own song. What is she going to do when she hears me rap my own lyrics? Get on the school intercom and tell the entire school I can rap!? When I get famous, I'm definitely putting her on my publicity team.

Back in class, it seems like the day couldn't go any slower. I feel like everyone is staring at me, and I'm unable to concentrate. To take my mind off of this awkward feeling, I start thinking about what Mrs. Harper said to me at recess. The "talk" actually got to me. Maybe I should tell my mom I like to rap. My dad may understand, and he can get my mom on board with it. Anything is possible.

Ring! Ring! Ring!

The dismissal bell is music to my ears. I'm walking super-fast through the hallways trying to leave school, hoping Kourtney doesn't catch up with me. I would run, but I know the teachers will yell, "No running in the halls!" So powerwalking is the next best thing. Just when I think I am able to ditch her, I hear her calling my name from a distance. I increase the volume of my music to drown out the sound of her voice. A few seconds later, she taps me on my shoulder. "Hey, Chase. Are you mad at me?"

"Yes," I say quickly.

"Chase, please don't be mad at me. I'm sorry for telling the class that you can rap, but I didn't like the things Jonathon was saying about you," Kourtney says exhaustingly.

"Whatever, Kourtney, I don't care anymore," I reply while walking away.

"Chase, you know how to rap, so why not let everyone at school see how great you are? When you get home, think about doing the talent show, and I will do it with you."

Kourtney and I walk the rest of the way home in silence. I have to admit, between Kourtney and Mrs. Harper's encouragements, I am starting to actually think about performing in the talent show. As soon as I finish my homework and chores, I am going to work on some music. But first, I need a snack. I deserve a snack after a long day.

Doing chores is sometimes annoying, but playing my music helps time go by quickly. Sometimes I even dance. It's six o'clock already? It's crazy how time works. At school, time was going slow, but now time is going fast! I can't believe it's time for dinner already. I feel like I just got home.

My plan of eating dinner fast and going back to the safety of my room lasts all of two seconds. As soon as I looked up from my plate, I see my mom and dad staring at me. Here we go, another talk!

"Your teacher called me today and said that you lost your recess because you did not want to share your journal assignment. Explain yourself," my mom demands in a soft, but serious tone.

My dad gives me a concerned look and says,

"Mrs. Harper said that you were supposed to tell your class about your talents. I am curious to know what your talents are, Chase. You have never told us."

"Umm, Umm, Umm..." I mumble in panic. They have me cornered.

"Stop stalling and tell us about your talents," my dad says.

"Music!" I finally yell out, surprising myself with how passionately I said it.

"What about music? Can you play any instruments? Do you like to dance to music? What is your talent?" my mom asks with encouraging excitement.

"I like to write songs."

"Wow, that is great! Baby girl, you know I was a lead vocalist in a band. Do you know how to sing?" my dad continues with a proud look in his eyes.

I pray they will change the subject. I am not ready to tell my parents I know how to rap. Now I know how DJ Jazzy Jeff and The Fresh Prince felt when they wrote their song "Parents Just Don't Understand." Instead of telling them yes, I silently answer his question by nodding my head up and down. I am not lying because I do know how to sing, but I am better at rapping.

"This is fantastic!" my mom screams. "You know, Chase, singing is a great talent to have. It was your father's voice that caught my attention. I fell in love with him and all it took was one song. Honey, can we hear you sing?"

Wow, my mom must really like singing because I have never seen her so excited! She has never told me the story of how she and my dad met. Between feeling embarrassment, and my face turning red, I do not know what to do. How do I get myself out of this? I am not ready to tell them I rap, but I don't want to lie either.

"*Think Chase, think*," I urge myself. Before I can catch myself, I blurt out. "Can I surprise you at the school talent show?"

My parents' faces light up with excitement, while my brother is banging his hands on the table cheering, "Chase sing! Chase sing!"

If there was ever a time I wanted to tell Chandler to shut up, it would be now. Instead I give my brother the meanest look possible, hoping it might do the trick.

"Yes, we would love to hear you sing in

the school talent show," my mom says with excitement. "When is the talent show?"

"It's next Friday. May I be excused from the table so I can work on my song for the talent show?" I ask in an attempt to end the conversation as fast as I possibly can.

"Yes, baby girl, go practice! I am so proud of you!" my dad exclaims with a huge smile on his face.

That was close. It seemed like I was never going to escape from the table. I put on my headphones and start playing some instrumentals beats I can write to. I instantly see myself standing on stage with a mic, Kourtney as my background dancer, and the crowd cheering for me.

The words of Mrs. Harper keep repeating in

my head, "It's time for you to stop hiding behind your notebook and let everyone get to know the real Chase."

5

On The Spot

Today feels different. The sun is shining through my window. The smell of bacon is in the air. So far it seems like today is going to be a good day. Surprisingly, I can't wait to get to school. When I look out the window, I see Kourtney standing on the sidewalk in front of my house. She is outside earlier than usual, and she looks like she is waiting for me. As soon as I open the door, Kourtney yells out, "So, have you made a decision about the talent show?"

"I am going to do it!" I say while rolling my eyes and smiling with embarrassment.

"Yes! It's on! It's on!" Kourtney screams while dancing in circles.

Kourtney is showing me all these dance moves she wants us to do in the talent show. She knows all the popular dances, and I hope I am able to do them all. As excited as I am, I'm still in disbelief I am rapping in the talent show. I can't help but begin daydreaming again. I'm standing on stage with a mic in my hand, Kourtney as my background dancer, and the crowd is cheering. Everything is in slow motion.

There is definitely something different about today. As I walk inside the school, I notice everyone staring at me. It's weird because people don't usually acknowledge that I exist. Having all these eyes on me is suspicious and terrifying. Could it be that mean Jonathon has been talking about me? Oh God, please do not let today be like yesterday. If it is, there is a chance I might run out of the school and never come back.

Like yesterday, the day is once again passing by slowly. Sitting in this classroom and watching people stare at me is making me sick to my stomach. I am ready for recess just so I can get some air. Kourtney passes a note over to me, asking me if I notice everyone staring. Now I know it's not just me. It is official. In the words of Kevin Hart, "It's about to go down."

Ding! Ding! Ding!

Finally, the recess bell goes off. As soon as Kourtney and I walk outside, we immediately start talking about the talent show. Kourtney has some great choreography ideas for the dancing. In her excitement, she is all over the place. She wants us to jump up and down, drop to the floor, and spin in circles. I can't help but laugh, and I am surprised that she has convinced me to do all these moves. Kourtney is teaching me how to do something calls the swing. As I spin around, I see Jonathon and his crew of friends, Frankie, Seth, T-Jay, and Mike, walking towards us. My heart is beating fast, and I am expecting them to give me a hard time.

"So, I hear you're going to rap in the talent show!" Jonathon scowls with his arms crossed.

How does Jonathon know that I am going to rap in the talent show? I instantly remember that Kourtney has a big mouth and probably told everyone.

"You will see at the talent show!" I reply in a

sassy tone. *I cannot believe I even said that,* I think to myself. I am completely stepping out of my comfort zone today.

"Well, okay smart mouth! I want to hear you rap right now! Bust out a flow for us, or are too you scared?"

I knew there was something weird about today. The universe has shifted, and bad luck is following me. First, my parents are drilling me about singing at the dinner table last night! Then everyone is staring at me in class, as if I had something on my face, but people are too afraid to say anything. Now Jonathan is calling me out to rap! What is going on today? All I can do is stand still nervously. I notice more and more people walking towards us and forming a circle around us. Is this really happing to me or am I dreaming? I can hear Kourtney in the background yelling, "Rap, Chase, you can do it! Rap the song you were rapping when we were walking home!" Every time I think about that song, "It Takes Two," by Rob Base and DJ E-Z Rock, I get excited. The surrounding crowd is chanting, "Rap! Rap! Rap! Rap!"

And before I knew it...

"I wanna rock right now!

I'm Lil Chase, and I came to get down!
I'm not internationally known!
But I'm known to rock the microphone!"

Just when I start getting into the flow, the bell rings to go inside. Everyone is cheering and loving the song I'm rapping. They don't know anything about old school hip hop. Some of them know it's an old school song, but some have no idea what I am rapping. They probably think I made it up. The next time they hear me rap, it will be to my own lyrics, so everyone can know just how talented I am. I won't be caught off guard. Wait a minute, did I just say "next time!?"

* * *

Everyone is walking into the classroom with excited energy. People are pumped and hyping me up. I am the topic of everyone's conversation. Mrs. Harper looks at me, and winks with a big smile on her face. She turns around and yells, "Calm down everyone, recess is over!" Her wink means that I did exactly what she wanted me to do. I guess "the talk" paid off after all.

The rest of the day goes by quickly. To my surprise, I can't wait until school is over. My adrenaline is rushing, and I am ready and eager to rap again. Rapping in front of everyone was a mixture of excitement and fear. If I am able to rap on the spot, I can definitely rap in the talent show! Especially after I practice some more. Now I'm feeling more confident than usual, and I am ready to take over the stage.

During journal time today, Mrs. Harper lets everyone free write. I am using my time to write a new rhyme, so I can have something to rap about. I have a feeling that everyone is going to want me to rap again, so I need to be prepared.

Ding! Ding! Ding!

It is four o'clock and time to head home. As Kourtney and I are leaving school, she can't stop talking about recess. Seeing how the crowd responded to my rap has Kourtney excited. We decide today will be a great day to practice for the talent show. As we are walking home, I look back and see Jonathon and his friends behind us. Next thing I know, more and more people start following us too. Jonathon and his friends are popular, so wherever they go, everyone goes. Well except for me.

"Hey, Chase! You are not too bad. I see you have swag. There is one problem with the verse you rapped. That song is by an old famous rapper. My parents listen to that song all time. A real rapper has their own rhymes," Jonathon sneers with a smirk on his face.

His friends agree yelling out, "Yeah!"

Everyone is staring at me and laughing, but this time, I refuse to be embarrassed by Jonathon. I am going to show him exactly what I am working with. I took a deep breath, while walking right up and staring Jonathon in the face. "Okay Jonathon, you asked for it!" I announce while slamming my backpack on the ground.

"My name is Chase!
I take my place!
I regulate!
Every single day!

I'm the MC!
You always envy!
The new hottest thing!
You'll never forget me!

So Jonathon, take a seat!
Let me school you homeboy!
Or do you want to compete!?

Chase is the baddest!
You don't want this!
I bring the madness!
You can't touch this!

Yes, I'm shy!
Times have changed!
I'm now confident!
And ready for the stage!

So are you down with me!
Or are you an enemy?

Either way it goes!
I'm following my destiny!" ♪

Jonathon is standing there speechless. I've never seen him speechless before. He always has something smart to say. That means I did it. I shut it down. Everyone is chanting, "Go Chase! Go Chase! Go Chase!"

I look out the corner of my eye, and I see Jonathon's friend Seth looking at me so weird, a smile on his face. Kourtney is dancing around yelling, "That's my friend," over and over.

Everyone is watching Jonathon and waiting to hear what he has to say in response. To my surprise, Jonathon reaches his hand out for me to shake and says, "Not bad." I can't believe it, but just when I started to think Jonathon might have a nice side... "But you are not going to win the talent show with that rap!" Jonathon announces while walking away.

Not everyone agrees. People are telling me how much they loved my rap and they cannot wait to see me perform in the talent show. No one is even walking home with Jonathon because everyone is still surrounding me. Today is a strange day, and it keeps getting stranger.

Kourtney whispers in my ear, "Oh my gosh, Chase! Seth is walking over here to talk to you."

"You are amazing!" Seth says to me with a big smile on his face.

"Amazing? Wow, that is a first!" I reply awkwardly.

"Since we live by each other, can I walk you home?"

"Sure."

"Can you rap some more as we walk home?"

"Yes, I can." I decide to rap songs everyone knows, so we can all rap together. I also didn't want to reveal all the lyrics I have. Seth is cute, but I know for a fact he is going to be in the talent show with Jonathon, and I can't have Jonathon and his crew stealing my ideas.

6

Busted

The walk home feels like it ended as quickly as it started. Seth made sure Kourtney and I made it home. Just two days ago, Seth acted as if I didn't exist, and now he is walking me home. Wow, I guess revealing your talent makes you a lot more visible.

Just when I think things cannot get any weirder, I see my mom peeking out the window. I say goodbye to Kourtney and Seth and run into the house. As I walk inside, my little brother screams, "Chase has a boyfriend!"

My dad passes by me and says, "She better not!"

All I can do is smile, or should I say blush? Fifteen minutes later, my doorbell rings. It is Kourtney asking me to come outside. I ask my parents for permission, and their faces light up in surprise. They can't believe I am asking to go outside to hang out with Kourtney. They agree, but tell me I cannot stay out too long because dinner will be ready soon.

"It's Chase on the mic!" yells Kourtney.

"Shut up!" I burst out into laughter.

"That verse you did was hot. Jonathon was speechless, and Seth likes you!"

I can't stop blushing. I laugh to hide the blush of embarrassment.

"Kourtney, you should have Julia dance with you as my background dancers for the talent show."

"I sure will! Julia is the second best dancer in our school. We are going to make up the best dance routine ever."

"If Julia is the second best dancer, then who is the first?" I ask, making fun of Kourtney. She is so full of herself.

"Duh, Chase! I can't believe you asked me that. Everybody's knows that I am the best dancer at our school and in our neighborhood."

"Whatever, Miss Conceited. I am going to talk to the music teacher about the music, and I will give you a copy so you and Julia can make up some dances."

I've been outside for about twenty minutes when it's time for me to go inside for dinner. Before dinner, I have to take a shower. While showering, song ideas come to my head, and I lose track of time. My mom bangs on the door and yells, "Chase, are you alright?"

I turn off the water and yell, "Sorry, I'm coming out!" and rush out of the shower. I put on some clothes and start dancing around the house, thinking of the song I am going to perform in the show. My dad and my brother have a smile on their face, but my mom looks concerned. They are not used to seeing me act this way. I'm not even used to acting this way. I'm just so excited. When I sit down at the dinner table, I look up and I see my family staring at me. Admittedly, I burst into laughter.

"So, baby girl, tell us about your day!" my dad says with excitement and curiosity in his voice.

"It's was okay."

"Just okay? It had to be more than okay; you had a group of kids walking with you after school. A little boy to be exact. You went out to play with Kourtney, and you are dancing around the house like you have ants in your pants. What is going on, Chase?" my mom asks with a mix of excitement and concern.

"I talked to Mrs. Harper, and she told me to open up and start making friends, so that is what I did, and now I have friends." I reply.

"I tell you to do that every day," my mom replies.

"That is great! How did you make all those friends in one day?" my dad asks.

"I told my classmates I am going to be in the talent show." This is the safest way out of the conversation. I am still afraid to tell them that I am a rapper.

"When is the talent show again?" my mom asks.

"It is next Friday, so I have a lot of practicing to do. Kourtney and Julia are going to be in the talent show with me. Julia is Kourtney's friend from a different class."

"Great! Are they going to sing?" my mom asks.

"Not exactly, but it is a surprise, Mom."

"Okay," my mom relents, looking at my dad. She starts to change the subject. "I am going to the store tomorrow, so let me know what you want me to pick up."

It is quiet at the table for a few minutes, and then my dad begins to talk about his day. I am sitting at the table with a big smile on my face, thinking about the talent show. Before I can stop myself, I bust out a rap, not realizing where I am.

 "Hey mom and dad!
This is what I want for dinner!

I don't want no liver!
Or nothing bitter!

I want some collard greens!
Macaroni and cheese!
Please don't add no lima beans!

If you feeling happy!
You can give me a treat!

I want strawberry cake!
Or something sweet!

We can have ice cream!
Or yogurt on the side!

If you don't like cake!
Bake sweet potato pie!" ♫

It's quiet at the table for about five seconds. My rap came out like word vomit. My mom and dad's mouths drop, and they look utterly shocked. They are speechless, and they are never speechless, especially my mom. My little brother bursts out into laughter, laughing harder than ever. It sounds like he is choking. I have never heard my brother laugh so hard before.

"Excuse me, Chase Steward!" my mom shrieks in a tone I have never heard before.

"I... I..."

Before I could get my words, my dad interrupts me, "So, rapping is your talent, not singing?"

"Well, I... I..."

"Say what you are trying to say, Chase!" my mom shrieks again.

"I do know how to sing, but I am not that good at it. Rapping is what I am great at, and I love to rap. I am going to rap in the talent show,"

I explain in a mumbled whisper, the words coming out quickly as my face turns red.

"Is rapping the reason you have all these friends now?" my dad asks.

"Mrs. Harper told me to show everyone who I am. She said I should not be afraid to show my talent."

"I do not care what your talent is! You are not going to rap at the dinner table again. That is not lady like. In fact, you are not rapping in the talent show. You are excused from the table. Go to your room!" my mom huffs, while my dad is pointing for me to leave.

"Yes, ma'am." I sulk from the table with tears coming down my face.

*
* *

7

Defiant

This is crazy. I've never seen my mom so upset before. There was absolutely no way for me to prepare for the look that was on her face. It is all so much worse than I even imagined. Is she upset with me because I know how to rap, or is she upset with me because I rapped at the dinner table? Maybe I will never know, but thinking about it is not helping. I decide to practice the song I was going to do in the talent show in hopes of making myself feel better, but nothing is working. How I am going to tell Kourtney I can't be in the talent show anymore? Just when I get everyone excited, I have to turn around and disappoint them.

Beep! Beep! Beep!

The sound of my alarm is going off. I am not

ready to go to school and face the music. When I finally become visible and make friends, I have to disappoint them and go back to being invisible Chase. Time is moving in slow motion, and I already feel like things are going back to normal. As I wait outside for Kourtney to come out of the house, I see Seth approaching. If I run, Seth won't be able to ask me about the talent show. To my surprise, he just says hello and keeps walking.

Oh my gosh, the universe has shifted. Why didn't Seth stop to talk to me?

Chirp! Chirp!

"Have a good day at school, Chase," my dad says while unlocking his car door.

What a relief! Seth didn't stop because he saw my dad walking out of the house. A lot of the kids in my neighborhood are scared of my dad, which is weird to me because my dad is the coolest. Maybe it's a man thing. Kourtney came up to me dancing as she always does, with a big smile on her face.

"Kourtney, I got some bad news," I say in a soft tone, my head facing the ground.

"Oh no! What is it? Did Seth tell you he didn't like you?" Kourtney replies with a laugh.

"No, that's not it.

"So he does like you?" Kourtney presses the subject.

"Kourtney, that is not at all what I am trying to tell you. I can't rap in the talent show. My mom said I am not allowed to rap."

"That is messed up, Chase! Did she say why?" Kourtney replies with a confused look on her face.

"No, she didn't, but she got mad at me because I started rapping at the dinner table about what I want for dinner."

Silence hung in the air for a second, but then Kourtney bursts out into laughter. To my surprise, I start laughing too. Now that I have said it out loud, it does seem crazy.

"Chase, you might be worse than me. My parents get mad at me because I am always dancing around the house and all they hear is bumping sounds from upstairs. But my parents know that I love to dance. They may yell at me, but they get over it. Your parents are pretty cool. They will get over it," Kourtney reassures me while she continues to laugh.

"You really think they will? You didn't see my mom's face," I reply with a sad look.

"Girl! Yes! My parents look at me mean all the time. They take stuff away from me then give it back. Parents are weird like that. That's just how parents are. Sometimes they don't understand us, but they usually get on board."

Wow! I knew Kourtney was smart, but she is giving me wisdom right now. Maybe I need to start talking to her more often. She is like a dancing therapist. It's official, Kourtney is going to be on my marketing team when I get famous.

"You know what, Kourtney, you are right!" I exclaim with excitement.

"If your parents don't let you rap, maybe you can just dance. You, me, and Julia can do a dance piece together. I know you've got some moves. Besides, Seth is dying to see you do something in the show," Kourtney continues, laughing hysterically.

"Cool! I'll do it, but we are going to have to practice because you and Julia can really dance, and I need to make sure I am on point."

"Well look at you, talking slang. You rapping at the dinner table, now you are talking slang. I guess rapping is changing you!" Kourtney says with a giggle.

I am excited. Maybe the universe hasn't

shifted on me after all. I may not be able to rap, but at least I can still be in the show, which is something I would've never done before. As we arrive at school, the other kids are hanging around the front entrance of the school, waiting for the bell to ring. Everyone is facing Kourtney and me as we are walking up to the school. Everyone is asking me to rap for them before the bell rings, but I tell them no.

As we walk into Mrs. Harper's class, there is a journal writing assignment on the board. The journal question asks: "If you could change one thing about your life, what would you change?" I really do not feel like writing my feelings, but I have to write something. My notebook is the only place where I can be real and be myself.

"If I could change one thing about my life, I would be normal. I would be able to hang with other kids without being shy or hiding behind my rhymes in my notebook. I would change my parent's thoughts about rapping. They would accept me for the way I am and recognize my talent. If I could

change my life, I would be able to rap in the talent show."

After writing that journal assignment, I instantly became mad. My parents may never accept my talent. What if Mrs. Harper and Kourtney are wrong? As soon as the bell rings for the next class, a light bulb goes off in my head. Everyone wants to hear me rap, not see me dance. I am excited to be in the show, but I am sad I can't share what I want to share with everyone. What if I tell my parents I am going to dance in the show, but when I get up there I rap instead? I am going to do whatever I want to do. If I want to rap, I am going to rap every chance I get. My great plan may come with some severe consequences, and the next place everyone would see me is at my funeral.

In math class, we are learning how to multiply fractions. They are the worst. Mr. Smith wants us to practice the multiplication problems on the board for review. He walks around the room and calls on people randomly to answer the questions. I hope he doesn't call on me because I am not in the mood to talk. Taking a nap sounds like a good idea right now. On second thought, the first problem is nine times four. I am going to answer that problem, and then he won't call on me later. I raise my hand to solve the problem. Before I knew it, I feel the rapping vomit happening again. Instead of giving the answer the way I am supposed to, I decide to rap the answer...

♫ "Thank you Mr. Smith!
For calling on me!

This is an easy problem!
Like three plus three!

Nine times four!
Equals thirty six!

I counted the multiples of nine!
To get it quick!" ♫

The entire class bursts out laughing. Some of my classmates are falling out of their chairs on the floor. I have to admit that was hilarious. They can't stop laughing. I cannot believe I just did that!

"Quiet!" Mr. Smith yells, scaring everyone out of their seats.

"That is ten minutes off of everyone's recess! As for you, Chase Steward, all of your recess is gone, and you will be serving after school detention."

My eyes open wide, and my heart is beating fast. I even begin to sweat. I've never gotten detention before, or into any kind of serious trouble. Everything just got real. Oh no, what are my parents going to say when they hear about this? My parents are really not going to let me rap ever again.

The rest of the day drags by slowly. Finally, four o'clock comes, and everyone is getting ready to go home. I turn around, and I see my mom standing in the doorway. My face turns red and my heart is pounding a million beats per minute. It's time to face the music.

8

Face The Music

"Chase, step outside. You better not go anywhere," my mom says sternly. I'm not used to getting into trouble, so I am officially scared. Maybe my parents will show me mercy since this is my first offense. Or maybe they won't show me mercy after what happened last night and now in the classroom. I might as well kiss my freedom goodbye and get ready for the chains.

It's been twenty minutes, and my mom is still in the room talking to Mr. Smith. Mrs. Harper even walked in the room to talk to my mom. It seems like their conversation is never going to end. I hear my mom yell, "Chase did what!?" Oh no, my life is over. Is this what it feels like when you are about to die?

The door opened and my mom says, "Let's go!"

I have never heard her use this tone before. My mom is silent the whole ride home, which is not normal. We walk in the house, and my dad is sitting on the couch with his hand out. I already know what he wants. I can't believe this right now. Are they really taking my music player away from me?

"Just so we are clear, young lady, you are grounded for two weeks," my dad says while walking away.

My dad never calls me young lady. Rapping has destroyed my life. It can't get any worse than this. Between getting detention, my music player being taken from me, being grounded, and my dad calling me young lady, it feels like the end of the world. The doorbell rings, and I look out the window. It's Kourtney. My mom is telling Kourtney that I'm grounded, and I will not participate in the talent show.

I do not believe this. Kourtney has a big mouth, and five minutes from now the entire school is going to know I am grounded and can't perform in the talent show. I wasn't ready to face the music when I got home today, but I am definitely not ready to face to music when I get to school on Monday.

The weekend passes, and I am standing outside the house and waiting on Kourtney as usual. I'm thinking about how the day is going to go. Seth walks past me and doesn't even speak. I turn around, and I do not see my dad or my mom. Oh no! It's already started. I am not ready to go back to being invisible again. Just when I thought things couldn't get worst, my dad walks out and tells me he is going to drive me to school.

"What!?"

We pull up to school, and I feel like all eyes are on me again. It's embarrassing enough that I can't rap in the show, but having my dad drop me off at school is humiliating. Everyone is scared of my dad, and I don't know if they are not talking to me because of him or because of me.

During recess, I am starting to see that things are back to normal. I am back to not existing since I am not rapping anymore. No one is talking to me, except for Kourtney. Even Kourtney is not talking to me that much because she has been practicing her dance with Julia. I decide to do what I always do, sit in the corner on the wall and write rhymes in my notebook.

The rest of the week went by fast. At home, I've never been so bored. I can't stop thinking about the talent show. I wish I was off punishment, and more than anything, I wish I was able to rap in the talent show. This show is my only chance of discovery. Okay, maybe I am exaggerating, but I really want everyone to see my skills. I am not afraid anymore.

It is the day before the talent show, while sitting in my room, and my parents open my door. They have a paper in their hand, but I do not know what it is.

"I see you are not Miss Popular anymore," my dad says with a smile on his face.

"Nope, things are back to normal. They only like me when I rap," I state in a sarcastic tone.

"It sounds like they weren't really your

friends. Friends should like you whether you have talent or not," he explains to me.

"We want to talk to you about your rapping. The day of your detention last week, your teacher gave me a copy of your journal assignment, and we are shocked that you feel like we do not accept your talent. Honey, we love that you are smart and talented. We think it is great that you know how to rap, but what we do not like is where you choose to rap. You have to know that there is a time and a place for everything. Rapping at the dinner table and in class is not appropriate," my mom chimes in.

"We love you, and we've decided to give you another chance. We'll let you rap in the talent show, but you have to promise us all of your raps are rated G, and you are not saying anything inappropriate," my dad gives me a wink.

"Oh, mom and dad, I promise! Thank you!" I say jumping up and down and giving them a hug at the same time.

"I have talked to your school, and they are going to allow you to participate in the show. You have to meet with your music teacher during recess tomorrow to give her your music, and show her what you are going to do. And baby girl, I hope you win!" my mom tells me with a big smile on her face.

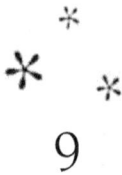

9

It's Show Time

Between the butterflies in my stomach and my palms sweating, I am so excited about the show. I finally get to show my family how well I can rap. The thought of me rapping in the talent show is surreal, and my parents being on board with me rapping in the talent show feels like a miracle.

Three hours have passed, and I have been practicing nonstop, and made up some dance moves to go with my rap when my dad yells, "Chase, time for bed!"

As Kourtney and I are walking to school the next morning, I decide not to mention the talent show to her because I want it to be a surprise. Kourtney also has a big mouth, and she will tell everybody. Trying to act normal is easier than I thought it would be. The whole school is excited about the show, and I have to pretend like I am not in the show. I can't help but wonder what everyone is going to think.

Four o'clock is finally here, and I am running out of the school as fast as I can to get home quickly and prepare for tonight's show! My mom is straightening my hair so I can wear my cap. My baseball cap has the letter "C" on it, which stands for "Chase." My outfit is some skinny jeans with my polo shirt that has "Chase" airbrushed in pink and white. I'm wearing my pink and white high top shoes and a pink bowtie. Dressing original shows that I am different. I am a nerd with swag.

As my family and I finally arrive at the school, I see a lot of cars outside. I get out of the car, and my family yells, "Good luck!"

I yell back, "Thank you!" smiling from ear to ear.

Kourtney is the first person I see when I get

backstage. "Surprise! I get to rap in the show!" I yell.

"Oh my gosh!" Kourtney and I scream at the same time.

"You look great, Chase! You are going to kill it, good luck!" Kourtney screams some more.

"You are going to kill it too. Good luck!" I reply while flipping my hair.

Jonathon and Seth's crew are on stage right now, and I cannot believe how great they are. For their talent, they are rapping and singing. Jonathon is the lead rapper, and Seth is the singer. I am starting to feel nervous again. Up next is Julia and Kourtney. Kourtney and Julia are going to do an excellent job, I just know it. Kourtney made up most of the routine. Julia and Kourtney's dance has the crowd cheering very loudly. The audience is absolutely loving them!

I am the last act to go on because I entered the talent show at the last minute. Butterflies are in my stomach, and I suddenly do not feel like going on. All I can think about is messing up and forgetting the words and the steps. But there is no turning back now, and I have my family out in the audience waiting for me to perform. They have to see what I've got.

My name is being called, and without thinking I feel myself walking on stage and hear my music start playing. The crowd is standing up, screaming, and clapping their hands. Everyone is yelling, "Go Chase! Go Chase!" In this moment, I feel such a rush! There are no words to describe the feeling. I cannot see my family because of the bright lights shining on my face, but I know they are clapping and yelling too. Before I can even think about all the people in the audience, my rap vomit reaches the surface and I am telling the audience to wave their hands from side to side. I am dancing to the beat, and my rhymes are flowing out naturally.

♫ Wave yo hands side to side!
Wave yo hands from side to side!

I am the new kid on the block!
Can't you see!
No other rapper can rap like me!

I may be shy and dress a little different!
But I am the girl you will always remember!

Shout out to Mrs. Harper!
For believing in me!
Because of you I can rap on this beat!

And to my friend Kourtney!
You are so cool!
There is nobody that can dance
like you!

Mom and dad!
You are the coolest parents!
I love how you came and made an
appearance!

To my brother Chandler!
You are so funny!
Your love is sweet like Texas Honey!

But enough about me and my peeps!
It's time to celebrate for victory!

Claps your hands and move from side
to side!
Now DJ let the beat just ride!

"When I say go, you say Chase!"

"Go!"

"Chase!" the audience screamed!

"Go!"

"Chase!" the audience screamed!

"Make some noise!" 🎵

I yell into the microphone as I walk off stage.

My performance is over, and it is time to announce the winners. The way the crowd is screaming, I get the feeling that I just closed the show perfectly. Even though I did a great job, the decision is ultimately up to the judges. Ms. Scale, my music teacher starts to announce the winners. In third place is Jonathon and Seth's group. I am shocked they came in third because they were so great. In second place are Kourtney and Julia. When Ms. Scale announced their name, I began to get nervous because I thought Kourtney was certainly going to win. She is the best dancer in our school. If Kourtney or Jonathon didn't win, then who will get first place?

"And the first place winner is... Chase Steward!"

I can't believe my ears. Did they just say my name? I walk on stage in shock. I grab my trophy, and I stand there smiling ear to ear. So this is what it is like to be a celebrity? Everyone cheering your name and taking pictures of you? I have to admit, I feel a little awkward, but I think I could get used to this. My dad is walking towards the stage with flowers. My mom is crying, and my little brother is laughing as usual. I'm surprised my mom hasn't fainted yet.

"Chase is cool!" my little brother says.

"Thank you, Chandler!" I couldn't help but giggle.

I'm happy a four-year-old kid thinks I'm cool, but I would love to hear that from someone my age. I see Seth and Jonathon out of the corner of my eye, and it looks like Seth is about to walk over towards me.

"Hi, Chase," Seth says.

"Hi, Seth."

"Congratulations! You deserved to win."

"Thank you! You guys did great. I didn't know you could sing like that!" I blush as the words come out.

"Thanks! Hey, everyone is going to Dave & Buster's tomorrow to celebrate. Do you want to come with us?"

Is this really happening? Am I really getting my first invite? I don't know what to say. I'm just standing here speechless.

"I have to ask my parents, but I would love to go!"

"Here is my number. See you later," Seth replies, passing me a piece of paper.

One thing I know from previous years, whoever wins the talent show always becomes popular. I know it is my time to shine. I will no longer be invisible Chase. I'm now the cool rapping girl. I can get used to this.

10

My New Life

It's been two weeks since the talent show, and I have been driving my parents crazy. Now that I don't have to hide my rapping skills, I rap all day and night. I can tell my parents are one second away from telling me to shut up. Until they do, I am going to keep rapping. My brother Chandler is laughing more than ever. He thinks it's funny that I rap. Now Chandler stays in my room all day because he likes when I rap to him.

It's amazing how one show turned my life around. I guess Mrs. Harper and Kourtney were right after all. They told me that my parents would come around, and they did. Mrs. Harper told me to open up and let the world see the real Chase, and now everyone likes me. I have to admit, Mrs. Harper gives good advice, and so does Kourtney. I truly believe anything is possible now.

My mom is so excited that I have a social life now. She is more annoying than ever because she wants to know everything that is going on. As usual my parents ask me questions about school, but now they are a little more extreme. At dinner, I try to eat my food as fast as I can. I don't think the awkwardness at the dinner table is ever going to change, but I am glad my relationship with my parents, especially my mom, has gotten so much better.

She is obsessed with my music! In fact, she is starting to act like those dance moms. Chandler and I call her the rapping mom. I don't have to hide my music anymore, which is exciting, but now every time I play my music, my mom comes in the room and asks me, "What song are you working on now?" Rapping has brought me and my family closer together. I am excited about the future and what it will bring. Just as I have this thought, I hear a knock at the door...

Knock! Knock! Knock!

"Chase, may I come in?" my mom asks.

"Yes, ma'am," I reply.

"Chase, I have a surprise for you. How do you feel about going to music camp?"

"Music camp?"

"I was talking to Mrs. Woods, Seth's mom, and she told me that she was sending Seth to this music camp, and I thought it would be great for you to go. The camp provides singing lessons, writing lessons, instrument lessons, and classes on the history of music."

"Wow, mom! I definitely want to go! Thank you so much!" I say excitedly, reaching out to hug her.

"I want to apologize to you for not being understanding of your dreams. Never think that I will not support you... I am one hundred percent supportive of your dreams. You have no idea how proud of you I am seeing you perform in the talent show. You were amazing, and I want you to use all the gifts that God has blessed you with. Because of you, I have a different perspective on rap music, and I thank you." My mom kisses my cheek, absolutely beaming at me.

"Thanks mom, and I know you are just being a mom. A crazy rapping mom," I say, laughing and moving to the other side of the room as my mom tries to grab me and hug me tight. Just when

I think things couldn't get any better, my mom tells me she is sending me to a music camp... and Seth is going too! I could just scream right now. This is going to be the best summer ever. I can't wait to tell Kourtney; she won't believe it.

As I wait for Kourtney to come outside to tell her the exciting news, I start thinking about how things have changed in just two weeks. School is definitely not the same. Everyone talks to me, and I have more friends to play with at recess. Now I like going to school. Not just to learn, but to socialize too.

"Hey, Chase," Kourtney approaches me.

"Hey," I reply, snapping out of a day dream.

"Guess what my mom told me yesterday!?" In my excitement, I don't give her a chance to respond and blurt out my good news. "My mom is sending me to music camp this summer."

"Great," Kourtney responds with a sarcastic tone.

"And Seth is going to the same camp!"

"Shut up!" Kourtney giggles. "Does Seth know you are going?"

"No, and don't tell him," I instruct her with a serious look.

"I won't, but you have to tell me everything."

By the time school is over, Seth will know about music camp because Kourtney has a big mouth. Seth hasn't walked to school with Kourtney and me since the talent show because he is afraid of my dad, and he is best friends with my enemy Jonathon. He is a boy of a few words when Jonathon is around.

It seems like school is going slow today, but I don't mind. Mrs. Harper is having us write a journal assignment about, "What do you want to be when you grow up?" Of course I want to be a rapper and songwriter, but I believe that I am already what I want to be. I may not be famous, but now that I don't have to sneak around to create my music, I am living the dream. Life can bring more possibilities, but right now I am what I want to be. I am a rapping girl.

Just as I think time is coming to a standstill, the last bell of the day rings for dismissal. I rush home to start my daily routine: making myself a sandwich and doing my chores. I decide to take a nap after I finish my homework. It was a long day, and I am sleepy.

"Okay, Chase, you and your parents sign right here on the contract," Ocean O'Neal says to me.

This is so exciting. Just when I think it can't get better than popularity at school, I am getting signed to a record label with Ocean O'Neal! My parents and I sign the contract. It is official, I am going to be a super star.

"The paper work is now complete. Welcome to HotSpot Records. It's time to get to work. Your album needs to be in the stores as soon as possible!"

Beep! Beep! Beep!

"Chase! Chase! Wake up and turn off that

alarm! Get ready for school," my mom yells at my bedroom door.

Well, a girl can dream right?

The End